THE
MAGIC
SPECTACLES

and Other Easy-to-Read Stories

by Lilian Moore
illustrated by Arnold Lobel

PARENTS' MAGAZINE PRESS   NEW YORK

For Rachel Brown—with love

Contents

14257

The Magic Spectacles

Little Hoot lived in a tall tree
in the woods. He was a baby owl.
In the very next tree lived Grandfather Owl.

Little Hoot liked to sit and watch
old Grandfather Owl.

"Grandfather Owl knows everything!"
said Little Hoot.

Day after day Grandfather Owl sat
in his tree, looking out at the world
through his spectacles.

Day after day the animals of the woods
came to see Grandfather Owl.

Mother Raccoon came
to ask about her little one.
Poor thing! He had the sniffles.

Grandfather Owl looked down
through his spectacles and told her
what to do.

Crow came to ask about a scary man
that was standing in Farmer Gray's corn.

Grandfather Owl looked down
through his spectacles and told Crow
not to be afraid. It was only a scarecrow.

Red Squirrel and Gray Squirrel came
because they had a fight about some nuts.

"I saw them first," said Red Squirrel.
"They are all mine!"
   "No!" said Gray Squirrel.
"They are mine. I saw them first."
   Grandfather Owl looked down at them
through his spectacles.
   "Did you find many nuts?" he asked.
   "Oh, yes!" said Red Squirrel.
   "Many, many nuts!" said Gray Squirrel.
   "Well, then," said Grandfather Owl.
"Gray Squirrel, you take one nut.
Red Squirrel, you take one nut.
And keep doing that
until there are no more nuts to take."
   "Oh," said Red Squirrel.
"That sounds like fun."
   "Come on, let's do it!" said Gray Squirrel.
   And they ran off.

Day after day Grandfather Owl sat
in his tree, looking out at the world
through his spectacles.

Day after day Little Hoot sat
and looked at Grandfather Owl.

"How can he know so much?"
thought Little Hoot.

"It must be the spectacles.
The spectacles must be magic!"

One day Little Hoot was playing
under the tree.

He looked up and saw that Grandfather Owl
was asleep. Then he saw
that the spectacles were slipping, slipping
down Grandfather Owl's face.

Down
    down
        down.

Plunk! They fell on Little Hoot's head.

"The magic spectacles!" said Little Hoot.
He put them on and flew back to his tree.
"Now I will know everything!" said Little Hoot.

Soon Woodchuck came by.
He wanted to talk to Grandfather Owl.

"Grandfather Owl is sleeping,"
said Little Hoot. "Ask me!"

"Well," said Woodchuck.
"I need a new home. I want to know
if it is better on the other side
of the woods."

Was it better on the other side
of the woods?

Little Hoot looked through the spectacles.

But the spectacles did not help him.

He did not know what to tell Woodchuck.

So Woodchuck went away.

Soon Brown Bear came by.

He wanted to talk to Grandfather Owl.

"Grandfather Owl is sleeping,"
said Little Hoot. "Ask me!"

"Well then," said Brown Bear. "Tell me
a new place to look for honey."

A new place to look for honey?

Little Hoot looked through the spectacles.

But the spectacles did not help him.

He did not know what to tell Brown Bear.
So Brown Bear went away.

Soon Rabbit came by. Kerchoo!
He could not stop sneezing.

He wanted—kerchoo!—to talk
to Grandfather Owl—kerchoo!

"Grandfather Owl is sleeping,"
said Little Hoot. "Ask me!"

"Kerchoo!" said Rabbit.
"How—Kerchoo! Kerchoo!—
can I stop sneezing? KERCHOO!"

How could Rabbit stop sneezing?

Little Hoot looked through the spectacles of Grandfather Owl.

But the spectacles did not help him.

Little Hoot did not know what to tell Rabbit.

"Kerchoo!" said Rabbit, and he went away.

"These spectacles are not magic," said Little Hoot. "They are not magic at all! They do not help me know anything."

Grandfather Owl was not really sleeping all this time.

Now he looked at Little Hoot and said:

Spectacles are for seeing
and not for knowing.
Knowing comes with
growing and growing.

"But I wanted to know everything," said Little Hoot. "The way you do!"

"Little Hoot," said Grandfather Owl, "you know everything now that a little owl has to know.

"When you are a grandfather owl,
you will know everything
that a grandfather owl has to know.
   "Now may I have my spectacles, please?"
   Grandfather Owl put on his spectacles
and closed his eyes.
And this time he *really* went to sleep.

13

The "Now Really" Time

"Now really!"

That's what mothers were saying
all over town.

"Now really, Susan, have you lost
a mitten *again?*"

"Now really, Michael Lee, where *is*
your new red scarf?"

"Now really, Elizabeth Ann, don't tell me
you can't find your good blue gloves!"

You could tell the mothers were cross.
They said Susan instead of Susie,
and Michael Lee instead of Mike.

The mothers were cross, but the children
were having fun.

They lost so many things
because they were out playing so much.

And they were out playing so much
because of the snow.

15

Never had they seen such snow.
It kept coming down, down, down.

Never had snow seemed so white or so soft.
Never had it seemed so right for snowballs
and snowmen, for sleds and for forts.

Best of all, Big Hill had never been
so much fun before.

Big Hill was right outside the town.
It was a hill that rose gently,
and went right up into the woods.
Everyone said that Andy Miller was lucky
because the hill was right behind his house.

It was fun to play on Big Hill at any time.
But now the children came to play there
every day.

They walked up the snowy hill—puff, puff, puff.
They rode down on sleds. Look out below!
But the days were colder.
Colder and colder.
Noses were getting redder.
Feet were getting so cold that they hurt.
One day it was so cold that only
two big boys came out to play on Big Hill.
They had a snowball fight.
One boy made a big fat snowball
and threw it at his friend.
He missed.
The snowball began to roll down the hill.
It got bigger and bigger.
Then it rolled up to a tree and stopped.
"Brr-rr-rr!" said the boys. "It's cold!"
And they ran home to get some hot cocoa
and watch TV.

Now it was very quiet on the snowy hill.
A hungry squirrel came out of the woods.
He was looking for nuts he had hidden.
He pushed at the snowball with his nose.

The snowball rolled away.

It rolled down the hill, getting bigger
and bigger. Thump! The snowball bumped
into a tree again and there it stayed.

That night a deer came out of the woods.
The deer stood by a tree, looking
and listening. Then he turned
and ran back into the woods.

As he ran he kicked the snowball
and the snowball rolled away.

It rolled down, down the hill, getting
bigger and bigger and bigger. Then at last
it came to a stop.

When Andy Miller looked out of his window
the next morning, he yelled, "Yippee!"

There in his backyard was a snowball.
But what a snowball! It was bigger than Andy!

All his friends came to see it.

Even the grownups came to see the giant
snowball that had rolled down the hill.

"It looks like something from outer space!"
cried Mike.

"Let's play satellite!" cried Andy.

So they put sticks into the snowball
and said it was Satellite X.

"Now let's make him the Man from Mars,"
said Susie.

They took an old bike tire and cut it up.
They took an old mop. They put a face
and some whiskers on the giant snowball.
Now it was the Man from Mars.

Day after day Andy and his friends had fun
with the snowball in the backyard.

Then the sun came out. The days got warmer.
Warmer and warmer.

Now when the children walked in the snow,
it got mushy under their feet.

The melting snow ran into the streets
in little rivers.

And the giant snowball began to melt.
Slowly, slowly, drip by drip.

Drip, drip through the day.

Drip, drip through the night.

One morning when Andy looked out of his window, there was no snowball.

He ran into the yard to make sure.

No snowball.

But all over the yard there were things.

There was a red mitten.

There was a red scarf.

There were blue gloves.

There was a brown rubber.

When the children came to play, they saw their things.

"We lost them on Big Hill," cried Mike.

"And the snowball brought them down!" said Susie.

The mothers were the most surprised.

All they could say was, "Now really!"

Janey's Boss

Boss was a crow, a big black crow.
He was Janey Fisher's pet.
Where did Boss come from?
"Out of the sky," said Janey.
That was true.
One day the big black crow
flew out of the sky into the backyard.
He flew down into the big old apple tree.
He looked around. And he stayed on.
Sometimes people said,
"Janey, is that crow your pet?"
Then Janey said, "Yes,
but he thinks I am *his* pet."
That was true, too.
Janey did not choose the crow.
The crow chose Janey.

One morning he flew right
into Janey's room. He sat on the bed
and looked at her. Then he flew over
and sat on her head.

"See!" said Janey's mother, laughing.
"You are the girl for him!"

Janey *was* the girl for Boss.

The crow wanted to be with Janey all the time.

It was funny to see him walking beside her.

Sometimes he looked at Janey as if to say,
"Why don't we fly, silly girl? Oh, well,
if you walk, I will walk, too."

24

Janey gave the crow his name.

Boss was his name, and bossy he was.

That crow did just what he wanted to do.

Did Boss feel hungry? He took
what he wanted.

Once the crow flew off with Daddy's supper.

How angry Janey's father was!

"You rascal!" he yelled up at the crow.

Did Boss feel like playing?

He took the toys he wanted.

One day Janey's brother Dick was working
on a puzzle.

The crow flew down onto the table.
He upset the puzzle
and flew off with a piece of it.

How angry Dick was!

"Oh, dear," Janey told her crow. "I guess
only Mother and I like you any more!"

Mrs. Fisher did like Boss—most of the
time.

Then one day she hung out a line full
of white clothes.

Boss came along and pulled off
all the clothespins. Every last one!

After that, Janey had a talk with her crow.

"Look here, Boss," she said. "I am going
to teach you something. When I say
STOP THAT, you must do what I say!"

Janey went around saying STOP THAT to Boss.
Boss did learn. But what did he learn?

He learned to say STOP THAT!

He loved to say it out loud again and again.

One morning the milkman was putting
some bottles of milk on the doorstep.

"STOP THAT!" someone said.

The milkman jumped back.

He looked around, but saw no one.
So he put the milk bottles back.

"STOP THAT!" someone said.

The milkman jumped back again.

Again he looked around and saw no one.
Again he put the bottles down.

Again he heard, "STOP THAT!"
  This time the milkman looked up
and saw Boss.
How angry the milkman was!
  "Oh, Boss!" said Janey. "Everybody is so
angry with you. Why can't you be good?"
  Boss flew to Janey and sat on her head.
  "STOP THAT!" said Boss.
And Janey had to laugh.

Then one day something happened. After that
no one was angry with Janey's pet any more.

Boss was up in the tree. He looked down
and saw something.

"STOP THAT!" he cried. "STOP THAT!"
out loud—again and again.

"STOP THAT!
STOP THAT!
STOP THAT!"

Mrs. Fisher came out of the house
to scold him.

Then she saw what Boss saw.

The baby next door was walking
out into the road!

Mrs. Fisher ran out and got him—fast!

What a fuss everyone made about Boss.
They made such a fuss that he yelled,
"STOP THAT!"

Where had Boss come from?

Out of the sky—just like that.

One day—just like that—Boss was gone. Some wild crows flew over the old apple tree. Boss saw them, and off he went— back into the sky.

It was a sad day for Janey.

"He was the best pet I ever had," she said.

"I know how you feel," said her mother. "I miss that old Boss, too."

That made Janey feel a little better.

"I miss the rascal, too," her father said at supper one night.

" So do I," said Dick.

That made Janey feel *much* better.

"Do you think Boss will come back someday?" she asked.

"Maybe," said her father. "If he wants my supper."

"Maybe," said Dick. "If he misses my toys."

"Most of all," said Janey's mother,
"Boss will come back when he misses his girl."

"When will that be?" Janey wanted to know.

"He'll come back when he wants to,"
said Janey's mother.

"After all, he's the Boss!"

The Pet that Benjy Wanted

Benjy Brown was eating his breakfast.
He was thinking, too.
Suddenly he said to his mother,
"I wish I had a pet.
I wish I had a pet more than anything!"
His mother looked surprised.
"What kind of pet do you wish for, Benjy?"
she asked.
Benjy thought about a dog.
But every time he thought about dogs,
he thought of Lady. Lady was Mrs. Miller's dog,
and she lived next door.
Benjy did not tell anyone, but he was
a little afraid of Lady.

Mrs. Miller said Lady was a good dog.

Maybe she was.

But she was so BIG.

And her bark was so LOUD. When she barked
she made Benjy jump.

So Benjy did not say, "I wish for a dog."

He just said, "I don't know the pet I want.
I have to think about it.
I have to find out."

After breakfast Benjy walked
down the street to Mike's house.

On the way he passed the fish store.
In the window there was a big glass tank
full of goldfish.

Benjy stopped to look.

"It's so much fun to watch goldfish,"
he thought. "Do I want
some goldfish for pets?"

Benjy watched the little fish
going around and around in the big glass tank.

"No," he said at last.
"You can't hold a goldfish.
You can't play with a goldfish.
That's not the pet I want."

And he walked on to Mike's house.

Mike did have a pet. It was a little bird—
a little blue parakeet.

"Do I want a parakeet?" thought Benjy.

Mike let the little blue bird out of the
cage. It came right over to Mike
and sat on his finger!

"HI, MIKE!
HI, MIKE!
HI, MIKE!" said the parakeet.
Benjy laughed.

Suddenly the little bird hopped
onto Benjy's finger.

"Say," he thought. "This bird is funny.
Maybe I *do* want a parakeet."

Benjy and Mike played
with the bird.

It was fun to see it hop
from Benjy's finger to Mike's finger
and back again.

Then Benjy said, "Come, Mike,
let's go to Robbie's house."

"Wait!" said Mike.

He called to his parakeet. It hopped
onto Mike's hand, and Benjy watched as Mike
put the little bird back into the cage.

"No." Benjy thought. "I don't want
a pet that I have to keep in a cage."

Robbie had a turtle.
He called it Tillie-Turtle,
and Benjy always liked to watch it.

This time Benjy looked at Tillie-Turtle
and thought, "Robbie likes his turtle so much.
Do I want a turtle, too?"

Robbie let Benjy feed the turtle.

"Look at that!" cried Robbie.
"See the way she goes after that food!"

Benjy watched Tillie-Turtle eat. Snap! Snap!

He watched her go slowly over the rock
in her tank, and then slowly,
oh so slowly, back again.

"No," thought Benjy. "I like Tillie-Turtle,
but I want a pet that can run and jump."

All the way home Benjy kept thinking,
"I wish I had a pet.
I wish I had a pet more than anything."
    "Benjy!" said his mother.
"What a surprise there is! Guess!"
    "I give up!" said Benjy. "Tell me!"
    "Come with me and see," said his mother.
    Benjy went with his mother.
They went to the house next door.
    When Mrs. Miller saw Benjy, she said,
"Oh yes. I know what *you* want to see.
Come with me."
    "What is it?" thought Benjy.
"What is it I want to see?"
    Mrs. Miller took him into the house
and then to a little room.
    "Look, Benjy," said Mrs. Miller.
    At first Benjy saw only a big basket.
    He looked again, and all he could
say was OH!

And then OH! again.

There in the basket was Lady.

And there in the basket with her
were three new little brown and white puppies!

Lady did not look very big right now.

And the puppies were so little they could not
even stand up.

"Do you want one, Benjy?" asked Mrs. Miller.
"Do you want a little brown and white puppy?"

Then Benjy knew.

"Oh yes!" he said. "A puppy is the pet
I really wanted all the time!"

The Silver Bird Express

Toot! Tooooooooooooooooooooooot!

What was that?

Danny sat up in bed.

Toot! Toot! Tooooooooooooooooooot!

He knew that train whistle.

It was the Silver Bird Express.

Danny knew all the trains that went roaring down the tracks near his house.

For Danny knew what he was going to do when he grew up.

He was going to drive a train like the Silver Bird Express.

Toot! Toooooooooooot! Tooooooooooooot!

Come along, Danny. Cooooome aloooooong! the whistle seemed to call through the night.

43

"Not now!"

he called back to the speeding train.

"Not now. But some day soon!"

Danny closed his eyes.

Then all at once something happened.

All at once he was moving—fast!

Where was he?

Danny sat up and looked around.

He was sitting in a train, full of people!

Why, it was the Silver Bird Express!

How did he ever get here?

He looked at himself.

He had on his engineer's suit,

and in his hand he had his lunch box!

The Silver Bird was roaring down the tracks.

Faster and faster it went.

Then all at once it came to a stop.

And what a stop!

People fell out of their seats.

The girls screamed.

"What is it?

What's the matter?" everyone cried.

The engineer came running into the car.

"Is Danny here?" he asked.

"Yes, sir," said Danny. "Here I am."

"Can you help us, Danny?"
asked the engineer. "We are in trouble."

"What's the matter?" Danny wanted to know.

"There's an elephant on the track!"
said the engineer.
"And he just won't go away.
The train is very late."

"An elephant!"
the girls all screamed again.

But Danny ran out to take a look.

Yes, indeed, there was an elephant
sitting on the tracks.

It was a great big elephant,
and it looked as if it were just about
to take a good long snooze.

"Go away!" yelled the conductor.

"Go away!" yelled the engineer.
"This is the Silver Bird Express
and we are late!"

Danny did not say a word. He just
opened his lunch box and took out a sandwich.
A peanut butter sandwich!

Sniff! Sniff!
The elephant began to walk to Danny.

Sniff!

The elephant walked right off the tracks.
It walked right over to Danny
and took the sandwich.
   Everybody cheered.
Then they all hopped back on the train.
   "Thank you, Dan!" cried the engineer.
   "Isn't Danny wonderful?" all the people cried.
   "Full speed ahead!" yelled the engineer.
   Faster and faster
went the Silver Bird Express.
   Faster and faster—and FASTER.
   "Too fast," thought Danny.
"This is too fast, even if we are late.
Even if it *is* the Silver Bird Express."
   Just then the conductor came running.
   "Danny! Danny! Help!" he cried.
"The train is running away!"
   Danny ran to the engine room.
   "Help!" yelled the engineer.
"I can't stop the train!"

His face was very red,
and he was pulling as hard as he could
on the throttle.

"Help, Danny!" cried the engineer.
"The throttle is stuck!"

Danny took something out of his pocket.
It was a little can of oil.

Quickly he put some oil on the throttle.

"I use this on my electric trains,"
he told the engineer.

49

Then Danny pulled on the throttle.
He pulled and pulled and at last
the throttle pulled back.
Slowly the Silver Bird came to a stop.
"Thank you, Danny!" everybody cried.
All the girls tried to kiss Danny.
But Danny wouldn't have any of that!
He backed away, as far as he could.
Back—back—back—
Bop!
Danny opened his eyes.
Where was he?
On the floor of his room!
He had rolled right out of bed.
Danny shook his head.
"Boy, what a dream!" he said.
"What a dream *that* was!"
Danny got back into bed.
Once more he pulled up the covers.
Then far, far away in the night

he heard the train whistle again.

Tooooot! Tooooot!

"Not yet, you Silver Bird," said Danny.
"But don't you worry. Some day soon!"

Wait for a Windy Day

There was something that Red Fox wanted—
something he wanted very much.

Every day he came out of the woods
to look at Farmer Dilly's hen house.

Every day he thought, "My, how I would like
one of those nice fat chickens!"

Red Fox could get close enough to see
the nice fat chickens.

He could get close enough to smell
the nice fat chickens.

But he could not get close enough
to *take* one.

Not with old Trooper around.

Trooper was Farmer Dilly's big brown dog.
Every time Red Fox came near the hen house,
Trooper began to bark.

Every time Trooper began to bark,
Red Fox ran away.

Sometimes Trooper ran after him.

Sometimes Farmer Dilly
came out of the house with a gun.

So Red Fox always ran away
as fast as he could.

But the next day he would think again,
"My how I would like one
of those nice fat chickens!"

Back he would come to look
at Farmer Dilly's hen house.

Close enough to see those nice chickens.

Close enough to smell those nice chickens.

But never close enough to take one.

"That old dog knows. He always knows,"
thought Red Fox one day. "It must be
that he smells me. That's it! He smells
my fox smell when I come close."

Red Fox thought about that.

Then he laughed.

"Well, well," he said to himself.
"I think I can do something about that!"

Red Fox began to look around.

He looked until he had some good big bones—
the kind of good big bones
a big old dog would like.

"I will wait for a windy day," said Red Fox.
"Then I will give that dog something
to smell that is not a red fox."

He laughed, and thought of the
nice fat chicken that he would get at last.

Red Fox waited for a windy day.

At last a day came that was just right.

The wind went wooshing
through the trees in the woods.

The wind went wooshing
through Farmer Dilly's corn.

It was such a windy day that Mrs. Dilly said,
"This is a good day to dry my wash."

So she hung out her wash on the line
in the backyard.

She hung out Farmer Dilly's
long brown pants, and his gray pants, too.

She hung up all his blue overalls.
Then she hung out his blue shirts
and his good white shirts.

"There!" said Mrs. Dilly. She was very
pleased. "Now all my wash will dry."

Red Fox was pleased, too.

He sniffed the wind.

"Just the right day!" he thought.

He took the big bones and put them
on the path that went
from the farm into the woods.

"That dog will have a good time
in the woods today!" laughed Red Fox.
"And I will have a good time
in the hen house!"

This time Red Fox did not come
out of the woods.

This time he watched and waited.

The wind blew through the woods.

Soon it blew the good smell of bones
right to old Trooper's nose.

Sniff, sniff.

Trooper came running down the path.
His nose was on the ground.

Sniff, sniff, sniff.

The wind was full of the smell
of good big bones.

Sniff! Trooper ran down the path
into the woods.

"Now!" cried Red Fox.
"Now for the hen house!"

Red Fox ran out of the woods.

All he had to do now was run
across the backyard to the hen house.

Red Fox ran right to the backyard
where Mrs. Dilly's wash
was dancing on the clothesline.

Red Fox stopped.

What was that?

All those arms and legs!

Arms and legs moving all around!

Why, there must be a hundred men coming after him!

Red Fox turned and ran.

He ran until he was deep in the woods.

A hundred men! All of them coming after him!

"But I got away!" thought Red Fox proudly, "I got away from them all!"

Red Fox never did go back to Farmer Dilly's hen house.

Trooper still looks for the fox. "He doesn't come back," says Trooper. "He is afraid of me."

Farmer Dilly still looks for the fox, too. "He doesn't come back," says Farmer Dilly. "He is afraid of me and my gun."

How surprised Mrs. Dilly would be if she knew what really scared Red Fox away!

Little Will

Once upon a time there was a boy
named Little Will. He wasn't so little,
but that was his name—Little Will.

Little Will lived with his old grandma
in a little old house in the country.

They were very poor, but Little Will
didn't mind. Their house was warm and cozy.

"We are poor," Grandma said,
"but we do have a roof over our heads."

There was a little garden in back of the house.
Little Will and Grandma planted
beans and potatoes and cabbage.

They had one thin little cow, too.
Sometimes she gave them milk.

"We are poor," Grandma said,
"but we do have food to eat."
Little Will didn't mind
that they were poor. But nobody lived
near the little house, and he did mind
that he had no one to play with.

A road ran near the little old house.
Many people went by on the road.

One day Little Will was sitting
by the road. He liked to watch
the farmers go by with their wagons.

All at once he heard something.

"Tra-la-la. Tra-la-la," someone
was singing.

Little Will jumped up and looked around.
All he saw was a white cat.

"Tra-la-la. Tra-la-la," sang the cat.

"A singing cat!" cried Little Will.

He picked up the cat and ran into the house.

"Grandma!" he cried. "Look!
I found a cat that sings!"

"That's very nice," said Grandma.

"Please, may I keep her?" asked Will.

Grandma knew that Little Will
had no one to play with, so she said yes.

Little Will was happy with his singing cat.
He played with her every day.

The cat was happy, too.

She sang, and she ate.

She ate and ate and ate.

One morning Grandma said, "Little Will, we cannot keep your cat.
She is eating all our food."

Poor Little Will.
He knew Grandma was right.

He picked up the cat and said,
"Come. I will find you a good home."

Little Will sat down by the road with his cat at his side.

"Someone will come by," he told her.
"Someone will come by who can give you a good home."

"Tra-la-la. Tra-la-la," sang the cat.

Soon someone did come by.
It was an old man with a little brown dog.

The man saw Little Will and he stopped.

"Good day, sir," said Little Will.
"Do you want a cat that sings?"

"A cat that sings?" said the man.
He looked very happy. "You are just the one
I am looking for. Do you see my dog?"

Little Will looked at the brown dog.

"You have a cat that sings,"
the man went on. "And I have a dog
that can play the fiddle. Watch this."

The dog stood up on his back legs.
He put the fiddle under his chin
and began to play.

He played such a happy song
that Little Will began to tap his feet.

He played such a happy song
that two squirrels ran down from the trees
and began to dance.

"Why that's wonderful!" cried Little Will.

"I'm glad you like him," said the man.

"I have been looking for someone
who will give him a good home. He is yours!"

And he went quickly down the road.

Little Will could not wait
to tell his grandma. He went back
to the house, holding his cat
and leading his new dog.

"Grandma!" he cried. "Look!
I found a dog that plays the fiddle!"

He gave the dog the little fiddle,
and the dog began to play his happy song.

"That's very nice," said Grandma.

"Please, may I keep him?"
asked Little Will.

"Little Will," said Grandma. "We don't have
enough food for your cat. How will we feed
a cat and a dog?"

Poor Little Will.
He knew Grandma was right.

He picked up the cat again. "Come,"
he told the dog. "I will find a good home
for both of you."

Back he went to the road.

"Someone will come by soon,"
he told the cat and the dog. "Here!"
He gave the dog the little fiddle.

The dog began to play his happy song.

The cat began to sing.

The two squirrels came out of their trees
to dance.

Soon some farmers came down the road
in their wagons. They stopped to watch.
They laughed and tapped their feet
to the dog's happy song.

Soon more people came by.
They stopped to watch, too.

When the dog had played his song,
he made a bow. Then the cat made a bow, too.

Everybody laughed.

"It's a good show!" they said,
and they all clapped.

Then they took Little Will's cap
and passed it around.
Everybody put some money into the cap.
Little Will had never seen
so much money before.
He ran all the way back to the house.
"Grandma!" he cried.
"I have found a good home
for my cat and dog."
"That's very nice," said Grandma.
"And the good home is right here!"
said Little Will. Then he showed her
the cap full of money.
"My cat and dog can pay for their food,"
said Little Will proudly.
"We can put on a show every day, can't we?"
"Tra-la-la," sang the cat.
The dog picked up his fiddle
and played his happy song.

As for Little Will, he just grabbed
his grandma and danced with her
all around the room.

LILIAN MOORE is no stranger to the needs and problems of children's early reading. As a member of the Bureau of Educational Research of the New York City Board of Education, she worked for many years as a reading specialist, working with non-readers of all ages. She has contributed beginning reader stories to *Humpty Dumpty's Magazine* ever since it was started, and in addition has written many books for independent reading at the primary grade level. These stories all first appeared in *Humpty Dumpty's Magazine*.

ARNOLD LOBEL has been involved with children's books ever since graduating from Pratt Institute ten years ago, not only as an illustrator but as an author, too. *Prince Bertram the Bad,* and *A Holiday for Mister Muster* are perhaps his best known. Two years ago he illustrated *Miss Suzy* for Parents' Magazine Press. Mr. Lobel lives in Brooklyn, New York with his wife (who also illustrates books) and his two children, Adam and Adrianne.